Fusspot Bill

Written by
Hannah Welchman

Illustrated by
Jonathan Ball

Bill the bug is a fusspot.

Bill huffs and puffs.
Bill has no fun.

If the bed is a mess,
Bill gets mad.

If the bun is not big,
Bill gets sad.

If it is hot on the bus,
Bill gets off.

If Mum nags Bill,
Bill kicks his legs.

If Dad nags Bill,
Bill has a fit.

Bill has to nap on the bed.
But a dog is on the bed.

Back off, Bill! If a bug is on the bed, the dog gets mad!

The dog kicks Bill off the bed.

A fusspot bug
and a fusspot dog!